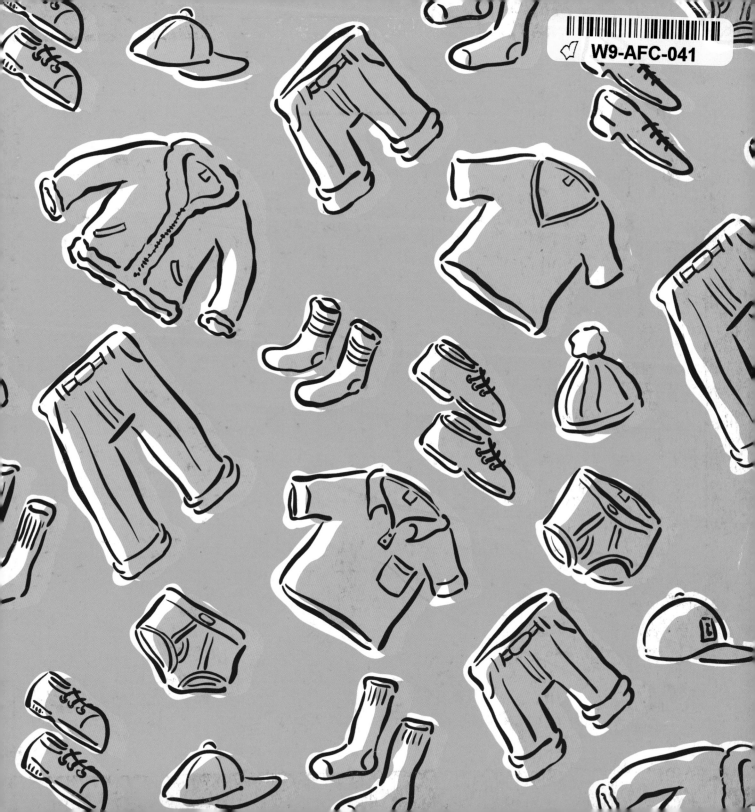

To Rollo, who always knows where everything goes. —R.V.

To my little boy, Sawyer. —C.R.

STERLING CHILDREN'S BOOKS
New York

An Imprint of Sterling Publishing Co., Inc.
1166 Avenue of the Americas
New York, NY 10036

ISBN 978-1-4549-1592-8

Distributed in Canada by Sterling Publishing Co., Inc.
c/o Canadian Manda Group, 664 Annette Street
Toronto, Ontario, Canada M6S 2C8
Distributed in the United Kingdom by GMC Distribution Services
Castle Place, 166 High Street, Lewes, East Sussex, England BN7 1XU
Distributed in Australia by Capricorn Link (Australia) Pty. Ltd.
P.O. Box 704, Windsor, NSW 2756, Australia

For information about custom editions, special sales,
and premium and corporate purchases, please contact
Sterling Special Sales at 800-805-5489 or
specialsales@sterlingpublishing.com

Manufactured in China

Lot #:
2 4 6 8 10 9 7 5 3 1
06/16

www.sterlingpublishing.com

Design by Irene Vandervoort

Where Do Pants Go?

by
Rebecca Van Slyke

illustrated by
Chris Robertson

STERLING CHILDREN'S BOOKS
New York

Where does underwear go?

On your chest?
No.

Underwear goes on your bottom.

That's where underwear goes!

Underwear on your bottom!

Where do pants go?

On your arms?

No.

Pants go on
your legs.

That's where pants go!

Pants on your legs,
and underwear on your bottom!

Where do shirts go?
On your knees?

 No.

On your hips?

No, no, NO!

Shirts go over your head
and onto your chest.

Shirt on your chest, pants on your legs,

and underwear on your bottom!

Where do socks go?

On your hair?

No.

On your ears?

No,
no,
NO!

Socks go over your feet and
up to your ankles.
That's where socks go!

Socks on your feet,
shirt on your chest,
pants on your legs,

and underwear on your bottom!

Where do shoes go?

On your hands?

No.

Shoes go on your feet.
That's where shoes go!

Shoes and socks on your feet,
shirt on your chest, pants on your legs,
and underwear on your bottom!

Where do hats go?

On your foot?

No.

Hats go on your head.
That's where hats go!

Hat on your head,
shoes and socks on your feet,
shirt on your chest,
pants on your legs,

and underwear on your bottom!

Where do jackets go?

On your face?

No.

Jackets go over your shirt,

And wrap around your body.
That's where jackets go!

Jacket over your shirt,
hat on your head,
shoes and socks on your feet,
shirt on your chest,
pants on your legs,
and underwear on your bottom!

Now where do these kids go?

Into the bathtub?

No.

To bed?

No, no, NO!

These kids go out to play!
That's where they go!
Kids go out to play
with jackets over their shirts,
hats on their heads,

shoes and socks
on their feet,
shirts on their chests,
pants on their legs,
and underwear
on their bottoms!